NEW SC
NO WAY!
BY BILLIE GOODE AND
DEVIN HARVEY
ILLUSTRATED BY:
FANNY LIEM

Love Clones Publishing
www.lcpublishing.net

Printed in the United States of America

First Printing, 2016

ISBN: 978-0692659298

Publishers:
Love Clones Publishing
Dallas, TX 75025
www.lcpublishing.net

Dedication

This book is dedicated to my son Devin and all of the little "Devins" out there afraid to try a new school.

"Your room looks great"!, says Mom. "You have all of your things put away. Good job Son! Are you looking forward to starting a new school tomorrow?"

"No"!, Says Devin

"Mommy, I don't want to go to a new school"!, says Devin.

"Oh Devin, says Mom. You will make lots of new friends at your new school. You'll see. It will be such an adventure".

"Now get some sleep Dear", says Mom. "You have a big day ahead of you tomorrow"!

"I don't want to go
to a new school"!,
says Devin. It will be
too scary"!

12
9
3
6
12
9
3
6

SIT DOWN!

"Mommy Mommy wake up"!, says Devin. "I can't sleep. I don't want to go to school. The Bully, the teacher and the school were all trying to get me.

"It will be ok Sweetheart", says Mom. "I promise. You will make lots of new friends and you will love it! Your teacher will be very nice and you will learn lots of new things".

"Now don't be afraid little one", says Mom. "Go to sleep and in the morning you will see that it is not scary at all".

12
9
3
6

"Time to get up Devin"! says Mom. "Rise and shine"!

"Now have a great day Sweety and I'll be right here when you get out of school"!, says Mom.

"Mommy Mommy, school was fun!", says Devin. My teacher Mrs. Franklin is very nice. She gave me a sticker for being good in class. I made lots of friends today. I can't wait to go back to school tomorrow!"

The End

Devin and his mom reside in Chicago, IL. Billie has been in the banking industry for many years and Devin is now 17 years old and will be going off to college soon. He is the middle child. Devin has had an adventurous childhood. At the age of 8 he was presented with the challenge of having to change schools. He was very afraid so he and Billie wrote a book to help him get through his fear.

Made in the USA
San Bernardino, CA
13 July 2018